**Other Cambridge Reading books
you may enjoy**

The Best Present Ever
Sally Grindley

Captain Cool and the Robogang
Gerald Rose

Bananas in Pyjamas
Morag Styles

Carnival
Grace Hallworth

**Other books by Irene Yates
you may enjoy**

Cave of Secrets

Joe and the Ghost

Kit and the Lady Kate

Ollie

Irene Yates

CAMBRIDGE
UNIVERSITY PRESS

Cambridge Reading

General Editors
Richard Brown and Kate Ruttle

Consultant Editor
Jean Glasberg

PUBLISHED BY THE PRESS SYNDICATE OF THE UNIVERSITY OF CAMBRIDGE
The Pitt Building, Trumpington Street, Cambridge CB2 1RP, United Kingdom

CAMBRIDGE UNIVERSITY PRESS
The Edinburgh Building, Cambridge CB2 2RU, United Kingdom
40 West 20th Street, New York, NY 10011-4211, USA
10 Stamford Road, Oakleigh, Melbourne 3166, Australia

First published 1998

Printed in the United Kingdom by the University Press, Cambridge

Typeset in Concorde

A catalogue record for this book is available from the British Library

ISBN 0 521 63944 1 paperback

They found the dog at the edge of the
woods.

At first they didn't think it was a dog
at all.

It was in such a mess, with its coat all
matted and grey with dirt, it could have
been anything. There were bits of stick
and burs and holly leaves sticking out all
over it. They couldn't even see its eyes
because its hair had grown so long and
straggly.

Zoe said, "I think it's a dog."

"It's not," said Tom. "It's some kind of wild animal."

"If it was a wild animal, Ben would be scared of it," said Zoe.

That was true. Dogs are frightened of wild animals, everybody knows that.

But Ben wasn't frightened of *this* wild animal. In fact, far from it. He pulled on the lead, and wagged his tail happily.

"It must be a dog," Zoe said. "Ben wants to make friends with it."

"It's not very big," Tom said. "Should we try and catch it?"

"I'm not sure," Zoe said. "It's probably got fleas and diseases and things."

The wild animal just stood there, looking at them. When they started to move away, it followed them.

"It might bite us," said Zoe.

Tom pulled a face. "But it might not. It's not even growling."

In the end, Ben settled the matter for

them. He sat down. Then he rolled over
on his back with his paws in the air. The
wild animal came up slowly to him, and
began sniffing. Then it began to make little
crying noises.

"I think it's hungry," Zoe said. "Let's try
and put Ben's lead on it and see if it'll
come home with us. Mum will know what
to do."

Tom slipped Ben's lead off.

The little wild animal just sat down and let him put the lead around *its* neck. And then, tail between its legs, it went home with them.

"What on earth have you got there?" Mum exclaimed.

"We're not sure," Zoe said. "But we couldn't leave it in the woods. It was crying. It wanted to come home with us."

"Is it a dog?" Tom said.

Mum picked the scruffy little animal up. "It's definitely a dog," she said. "But I don't know what kind. By the look of it, it's been out in those woods for weeks. The poor thing's starving!"

She put the little dog out onto the verandah with a bowl of Ben's meat and some water. It gobbled the lot without taking a breath.

"Poor thing," Mum said. "We'd better take it to the vet's and get it checked and cleaned up before we try and find out who he belongs to."

"It's a poodle," the vet said. "Underneath all this long, matted hair there's a very nice little dog. I'd say it's been running wild for a few weeks."

The dog had no collar on. There was nothing to tell them where it had come from.

By the time the vet had finished, they couldn't believe it was the same animal.

It was definitely a poodle. A nice creamy colour, not grey at all. The vet had clipped all the long hair away and now it had a curly coat, close to its body. Its tail stood up, proud and wagging, with a fluffy little pompom on the end.

The vet said, "I'd say somebody lost this dog a long time ago. And they don't seem to have made much effort to get him back. Most people phone us if they lose their dogs. But I haven't heard of a poodle missing from anywhere. One thing's for sure. Whoever he belonged to wasn't very bothered about him. You can leave him here if you like, and we'll try and find a home for him."

"Can't we keep him?" Tom asked.

"What about Ben?" Mum said.

"Ben's already made friends with him."

Mum gave in, like she always did. "Oh, all right. But we'll have to try and find out who he really belongs to."

"What are we going to call him?" Tom asked.

"Ollie!" said Zoe. "Because when we found him he had holly leaves sticking all over him."

It didn't take Ollie long to settle in.

"Lap dog!" Mum said, every time she sat down to watch the telly, and he leapt up onto her lap.

Ben seemed to take on a new lease of life himself. Instead of grumping around like the old dog he was, he played racing and chasing with Ollie. He rushed after sticks, rolling and leaping about as if he was a puppy again.

Ollie was a very clever dog. He learned his new name really quickly.

And he learned to do lots of tricks. Giving a paw. Playing dead. Stopping at the kerb. Everything the children could think of to teach him, he learned.

"He might have learned to do the tricks before," Mum said. "When he lived with his *real* family."

"Don't say that, Mum," said Zoe. "We're his real family now. You know what the vet said. Whoever owned him didn't really care about him."

"You don't *know* that, Zoe," said Mum. "And I'm sorry but you have to face the facts. Now, I'm going to put postcards in the shop windows. And if somebody comes for him, we'll have to give him up."

But nobody did come for Ollie, not even after the postcards.

Over the next couple of weeks, Ollie made himself so much at home that Zoe and Tom could hardly remember a time when he hadn't been around.

Every day the children took Ben and Ollie for a walk. But, without saying anything to Mum, Zoe and Tom had made a pact that they'd never walk Ollie past the woods again. Just in case.

The old man took them by surprise.

They were walking the two dogs on their leads along the path that led to the bus stop, past some old people's bungalows.

The old man was leaning on a stick looking along the pathway when suddenly he raised his stick in the air and shouted.

Ollie began to jump and bark with

excitement and, before Tom could stop
him, the dog had pulled the lead from his
hands and taken off in the direction of the
old man.

The little poodle leapt up and down at
the old man, making little crying noises.
Then he jumped to be picked up, and the
old man hobbled up the path, as quickly
as he could manage, with the dog tucked
under his arm.

The children stared, their mouths wide open. It all happened so quickly, they didn't have time to do anything before Ollie was gone.

"That man just stole Ollie!" Zoe cried. "We can't just let him go!"

"But he might have been his dog," Tom said. "And if he *is* what can we do? If he wasn't his dog, why would Ollie have been so pleased to see him? Why would he have gone with him?"

"But he didn't look after him, did he?" said Zoe. "He let him get lost in the woods . . ."

Tom's face drooped with sadness. "I know it doesn't seem right, but you know what Mum said. Ollie was never really our dog at all. He must have belonged to the old man. We'd better just try and forget him."

But they couldn't.

They managed for five days not to go

down by the old people's bungalows. Then, they couldn't bear it any longer. They just had to find out if Ollie was all right. And, anyway, Ben, who was obviously pining for his friend, just kind of seemed to drag them that way.

Ollie was sitting on the old man's window sill looking out. He wagged his tail when he saw them and began to bark.

"There he is!" cried Zoe. "He already looks hungry."

"I bet he hasn't been for a single walk since he went back either," said Tom. The old man's face popped up at the window. He didn't look too pleased to see them.

Reluctantly, Zoe and Tom began to pull Ben in the opposite direction.

But Ben wasn't having any of it. He could see his friend, jumping up and down in the window. He wrenched the lead from Tom's hand, raced down the old man's path, and hurled himself at the front door, barking like mad.

The door opened, just as far as the safety chain would let it. The old man peered out through the gap.

"What do you want?" he asked, suspiciously.

Tom could see the old man was trembling, as though he was scared. He marched down the path, trying to catch Ben who shot backwards and forwards in his excitement.

"It's all right," he said, "I'm only trying to catch our dog."

The old man frowned. "You shouldn't let him run over people's gardens . . ."

"It's not our fault!" Zoe piped up. "He saw Ollie in the window, that's all. And he wanted to play with him."

The old man poked his face out a bit further. He looked puzzled. "Play with him? Ollie?"

"Your poodle," Tom said. "We don't know what his name is really. We called him Ollie."

Suddenly, there he was! He pushed past the old man, squeezed out through the gap, and raced straight up to Ben. Ben leapt up, wagging his tail. Ollie's tail began to wag furiously too. The two dogs eyed each other. Then they started to jump and skip round each other, nose to tail, sniffing and woofing.

"Come here, Ben!" cried Tom.

But Ben wasn't going anywhere. All he wanted to do was stay exactly where he was, playing and skipping and sniffing with Ollie. And Ollie wanted the same. The two dogs danced about together, crazy with joy.

Tom, Zoe and the old man stared at them.

And then the old man began to laugh. "Well," he said, "*they're* pleased to see each other at any rate! I reckon you must be the ones who found my Kimmy when he got lost."

"Got lost?" said Zoe, bursting with indignation. "He couldn't just get lost on his own, could he? You must have let him go off!"

"Why should I do that?" the old man
said, almost fiercely. "He's the only friend
I've got in the whole wide world, my
Kimmy. Saved my life he did. Had a bad
fall in the house. Old legs just gave way.
It's not much fun being on your own when
something goes wrong. If it hadn't been for
Kimmy barking . . ." The old man shook
his head sadly.

Tom stiffened. "What happened?"

The old man's eyes filled with tears. "In the end somebody walking past heard the dog, looked through the window and saw me. They called the police. Two days I was there," he said, "and nobody knew anything. I could have been dead for all anybody cared."

"Kimmy cared, though," said Zoe. "He got help."

"When the ambulance came to fetch me, poor old Kimmy must have sneaked out of the gate. But nobody noticed."

The old man was kept in hospital for weeks, and when he asked about his dog, he was told not to worry. Everything was being taken care of, they said.

But when he came home, his dog was gone. "Thought my heart would break," he mumbled. "Life's not worth living without old Kimmy to keep me company."

The children were silent, looking down at their feet, the grass.

Suddenly, Zoe piped up, "Well, you can't walk him, can you? Not with that leg! But we can. And then you won't be left on your own for days on end – we'll come and see you when we come and get Ollie – Kim."

"Oh," said the old man. He paused, then he grinned. "Well, that sounds good," he said. "What do you think, Kimmy?"

They all looked around. But Kimmy wasn't there.

"Oh no! He must have got out again!" cried the old man.

"Don't worry – he's with Ben. We'll find him – he won't have gone far," said Tom. "And this time, we'll bring him straight back!"